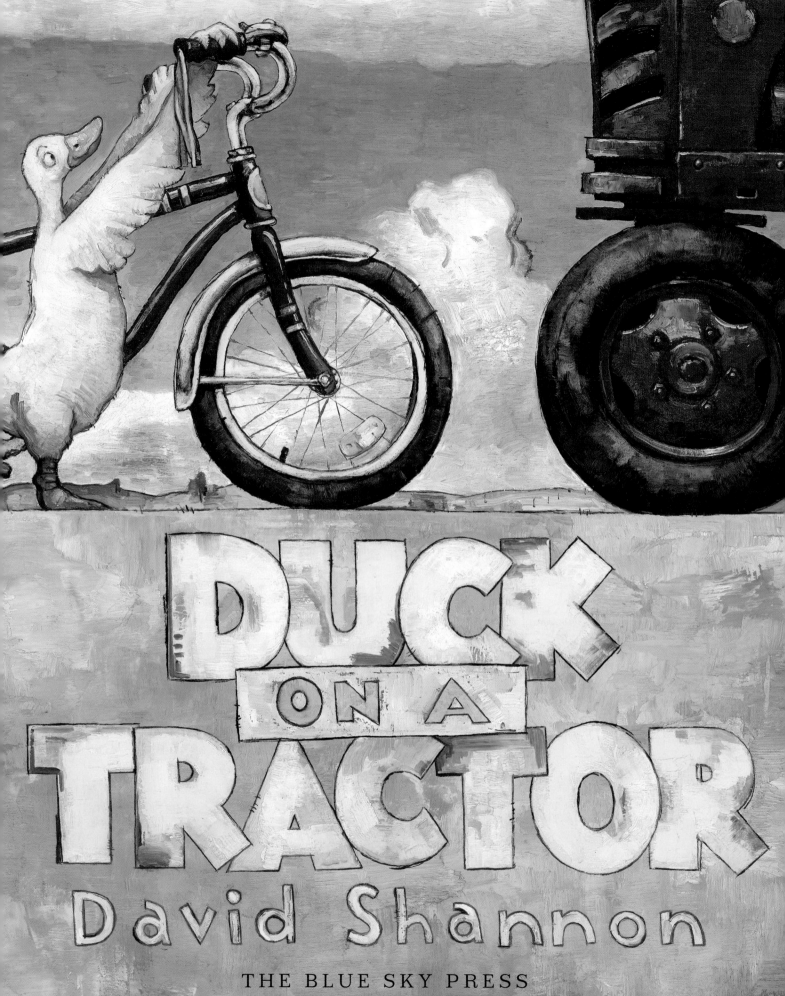

DUCK ON A TRACTOR

David Shannon

THE BLUE SKY PRESS
An Imprint of Scholastic Inc. • New York

Down on the farm, Duck sometimes got wild ideas. One day he decided he could ride a bike, so he did. Then he spotted the tractor.

"I bet I can drive a tractor," he said. The other animals weren't so sure, but they all said, "Well, if he can ride a bike, maybe he can drive a tractor, too!"

Duck climbed on the
tractor and looked around.

He pushed some pedals and wiggled a metal stick, but
nothing happened. Then a shiny little piece of metal
by the steering wheel caught his eye. He pulled it out.
He pushed it in. Then he turned it. . . . All of a sudden the
tractor shook and coughed and rumbled. It began to move!

At first it moved very slowly, and it jerked a lot, but it was fun! Duck drove around the barnyard until he got the hang of it. Then he stopped in front of the other animals.

"Climb on, everybody!" shouted Duck.

Dog was first. He jumped right up next to Duck. "Woof!" said Dog. But what he thought was, "We're going for a ride!"

To everyone's surprise, Cow clambered on next. "M-o-o-o!" said Cow. But what she thought was, "This is the silliest thing I've ever done!"

Pig and Pig took a seat in back. "Oink!" said Pig and Pig. But what they thought was, "This sure beats walking!"

Then came Chicken, Mouse, and Goat. "Squawk!" said Chicken. But what she thought was, "Last one on is a rotten egg!"

"Squeak!" said Mouse. But what she thought was, "I can see everything from up here!"

"M-a-a-a!" said Goat. But what he thought was, "I'm hungry. Does the garbage dump have a drive-thru window?"

Next up were Horse and Cat. Cat jumped up gracefully onto the tractor. Horse, not so much.

"Meow," said Cat. But what she thought was, "I was going to take a nap, but this should be *very* interesting!"

"Ne-e-e-igh!" said Horse. But what he thought was, "I think I'd rather walk."

The only one left on the ground was Sheep. "B-a-a-a!" said
Sheep. But what she thought was, "This is *too* dangerous!"

"Get on, Sheep!" everyone shouted, but Sheep wouldn't
budge. So Duck started driving away without her.

"Wait!" cried Sheep. "Don't leave me here all alone!"
She ran after the tractor and took a flying leap onto it.

"Quack!" yelled Duck. But what he thought was, "WAHOO!"

Duck steered the tractor down the lane
and out onto the main road. And
before long they were driving
right through the middle of
town. It was lunchtime, so
most people were in the
diner. They all looked
up when Duck and the
other animals passed
by the big window.

A little boy named Edison was having lunch with his grandma.
"Did you ever?!" Grandma gasped. But what she thought
was, "A duck on a tractor? That's impossible!"

"That's totally awesome!" Edison shouted. But what
he thought was, "No one's gonna believe this!"

Marcine the Waitress looked up from
her pad and noticed Cat. "Heavens
to Betsy!" she exclaimed. But what
she thought was, "I like cats."

Deputy Bob blabbered, "If that don't beat all!" But what he thought was, "How am I gonna explain this to the sheriff?"

A man named Otis chimed in, "I must be seeing things!" But what he thought was, "Oh, no—not *again*!"

"Holy cow!" hollered Manny the Cook. But what he thought was, "Holy cow!" (Manny usually said exactly what he thought.)

The Mayor almost choked on his pie. "Good gravy!" he sputtered. But what he thought was, "Those pigs are even fatter than I am!"

Corky just whistled. But what he thought was, "That duck is smarter than he looks!"

Gwen came out of the restroom. "Would you look at that!" she exclaimed. But what she thought was, "I can't see a thing without my glasses!"

Farmer O'Dell observed, "That's a dang nice tractor." But what he thought was, "Hey, that's *my* tractor!"

He decided he'd better go after it
and ran out the door. Everyone else
ran out, too, and chased after him.

By this time, Duck had turned onto the next street. The tractor shuddered to a stop. Duck tried turning the shiny little piece of metal again. Nothing happened.

"I don't know much about spelling," said Dog, "but I think that 'E' means it's the End of our ride."

Sheep cleared her throat. "Y'know . . ." she said, "I think we might get in trouble for this."

"Let's get out of here!" yelled Duck, just as Farmer O'Dell and everyone from the diner came around the corner. . . .

Everyone burst out laughing.
"Nah!" they all said. "It couldn't have been!"

"It was an optical illusion!" exclaimed Otis.
Farmer O'Dell said he must have left his tractor
running by accident.

"I guess that explains it!" Deputy Bob agreed.
Then they all went back to the diner
to finish their lunch.

And no one ever admitted that on that day,
they had seen a cow, a goat, a cat, a dog,
a sheep, a chicken, a horse, two pigs,
a mouse, and a duck on a tractor.

For Fergus

THE BLUE SKY PRESS

Copyright © 2016 by David Shannon
Library of Congress catalog card number: 2015030705   ISBN 978-0-545-61941-7
10 9 8 7 6 5 4 3 2   16 17 18 19 20
Printed in Malaysia   108   First edition, September 2016

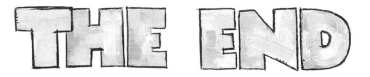

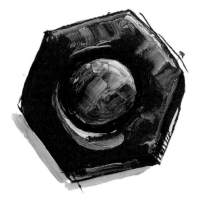